Walking Round the Garden

A Red Fox Book

Published by Random House Children's Books
20 Vauxhall Bridge Road, London SW1V 2SA

A division of The Random House Group Ltd
London Melbourne Sydney Auckland
Johannesburg and agencies throughout the world

3 5 7 9 10 8 6 4 2

First published in Great Britain by The Bodley Head Children's Books 1997

Red Fox edition 2001

Printed in China

THE RANDOM HOUSE GROUP Limited Reg. No. 954009

www.randomhouse.co.uk

ISBN 978 1 782 95463 7

Walking Round the Garden

JOHN PRATER

RED FOX

Walking round

the garden,

Like o

teddy bear,

One step.

two steps,

Tickle you

under there.

Walking down

the hallway,

Up and up

the stairs,

One step,

two steps,

What a

clever bear!

Sitting in

the bedroom,

What a

sleepy ted,

All I need is

a goodnight kiss

Then tuck

you into bed.